The Shadow on the Stairs

by

Ann Halam

First American edition published in 2012 by Stoke Books,
an imprint of Barrington Stoke Ltd
18 Walker Street, Edinburgh, United Kingdom, EH3 7LP

www.stokebooks.com

A catalog record for this book is available from
the US Library of Congress

Distributed in the United States and Canada by Lerner Publisher
Services, a division of Lerner Publishing Group, Inc.
241 First Avenue North, Minneapolis, MN 55401
www.lernerbooks.com.

ISBN 978-1-78112-015-6

Printed in China

Contents

Chapter 1
The House on the Corner

"Your house is haunted," said Emma.

"Don't be stupid," said Joe.

Emma was one of Joe's friends at school. They were on the bus going home and they were sitting at the back. It was their favorite place, but they didn't usually manage to get it because the Sophomores always grabbed the best seats. This afternoon their school bus was quieter than usual, because a lot of the older kids were away on a school trip.

"No, it's true," said Emma. "My aunt used to live on your street. She's told me about that house, the one on the corner. The one where you live. It's been haunted for years and years. If you step on the ghost's shadow, you are doomed. If it looks at you, you'll die."

"I don't care," said Joe. "I'm not scared of ghosts, anyway."

Joe's mom and dad had split up. He lived with his dad now. They'd recently moved out of their apartment and into a house.

When he got off the bus Joe walked down the street where he lived and stood looking at his house. It was winter, so it was already getting dark. The house was tall and thin, with little old-fashioned windows and chimneys that looked like skinny oversized flowerpots.

He wondered if Emma's story could be true. Joe's bedroom was on the top floor of the tall, thin house. There was a flight of stairs outside his door that led to the attic. Joe's dad was planning to do something up there, maybe make a workshop for himself and an extra bedroom, but at the moment those rooms were empty.

That night when he went to bed Joe stood outside his room and looked up the attic stairs. There wasn't any carpet on them yet, they were bare wood. He was wondering about Emma's story about the ghost. If there was a creepy place in the house, this was it.

The old staircase was narrow, and there were no windows in the walls on either side. In the light from the landing Joe could see a fuzzy shadow lying on the pale wood of the steps, about half way up. As he stared it seemed to grow sharper and darker, until it looked exactly like the shadow of a small person. Except that there was nobody there.

Joe felt frightened. It was only a shadow, but somehow it looked evil. Yet he was strangely tempted to go and tread on that dark outline.

"Don't be ridiculous," he said to himself, out loud. "There's nothing there." His voice sounded weird and echoey, in the silence at the top of the old house. But he wasn't going to get scared of a shadow, even if there didn't seem to be anything causing it.

Emma liked making things up. She often told whoppers. He would bet she'd never *had* an aunt who had lived on this street. She'd probably made up the story of Joe's house

4

being haunted, right there on the bus.

He decided he would put the ghost idea out of his mind. He would concentrate on the good things about moving, like having more space for all his things. He was planning to decorate his own room, and make it look really good.

Chapter 2
Diane

Joe got along well with his dad's girlfriend Diane. She was pretty and he liked the way she dressed and the way dad always seemed to be in a good mood when she was around. He also liked the way she didn't try to take over Joe's life.

Dad had had other girlfriends who were pushy, and worked too hard at being friends with Joe, or else they made him feel unwanted.

Diane wasn't like that. When she came to visit, life went on as normal. If Joe went off to his room to listen to music or play the latest soccer game on his Playstation, that was fine. If Joe and Dad wanted to do things together, the way they often did, she wasn't offended.

It was a big shock when he found out what was going on. It was a Saturday, a few weeks after they'd moved into the new house. Joe was still thinking about what Emma had said about the ghost. Every night, he looked for that shadow on the attic stairs. Sometimes he thought he could see it, sometimes he thought he couldn't. He told himself he wasn't scared but he wished he could get the idea that it was evil out of his mind.

He didn't suspect that something much worse than seeing a strange shadow was about to happen to him.

****

It started out by being a really good
Saturday. In the morning Joe was playing in a
match for his under-fifteens soccer team. Dad
and Diane both came and watched, and Joe had
a good game. He did some excellent tackling,
and he set up the team's striker for the
winning goal. It felt great to be playing well
with two people cheering for him on the
sideline.

In the afternoon Joe went over to his friend
Mark's house. When he came home, Dad and
Diane were in the kitchen, obviously preparing
a special meal. They had a bottle of wine open.

Joe looked at the wine, and the fancy food,
and Dad and Diane's smiling faces. Suddenly,
although he still didn't know why, he had a bad
feeling. Those smiles were too big and bright.

The three of them sat down to eat together, with a tablecloth and the best china and the good knives and forks.

That's when they told him. Diane was coming to live with Joe and his dad. She was going to move in straight away, it was all fixed up.

"Why didn't you tell me before?" demanded Joe.

Diane and his dad gave each other a worried look.

"We thought it would be better to get everything taken care of first ..." said Dad.

"You didn't tell me because you knew I'd hate to have her move in," shouted Joe.

"Joe!" snapped Dad, looking horrified. "Don't talk like that!"

"We don't need *her*!" shouted Joe. "We can take care of ourselves! Why do we have to have a stranger moving in? How could you do this to me, Dad? I hate you!"

Joe shoved back his chair and stood up. He moved too fast and accidentally pulled on the tablecloth. Everything went flying – food and plates and glasses.

Joe stood there, looking at Diane's shocked face and Dad's angry face. A huge stain of red wine spread over the white tablecloth, that was now lying in a crumpled heap on the floor at his feet. He hadn't meant to do it, but the whole mess looked exactly the way he felt, shattered and confused and twisted up inside.

He ran out of the room and straight up to his bedroom, and slammed the door.

After a few minutes he heard footsteps. His dad knocked on the door and said in a gentle voice, "Joe, come down and talk about it. I'm sorry we gave you a shock."

"Leave me alone," said Joe. "I'll be all right. Please, leave me alone for a while."

After a few more minutes, the footsteps went away.

Chapter 3
A Shattered Dream

Joe's mom had married again. She lived nearby, and Joe often went to see her. He stayed with her when his dad had to be away overnight for work.

He knew she loved him, but he felt like she was not really 'Joe's mom' anymore. She had a new life, and a new family. It was as if she'd turned into someone else. When he went to stay with her he had to share with his stepbrother. He didn't have a room of his own, and that made him feel he didn't belong.

He had felt safe with his dad. He'd believed that they would live together and look after each other until Joe grew up. He would always have a place where he belonged. Now that dream was shattered.

He sat on his bed thinking how stupid he had been. He should have guessed what was happening from the first moment Dad said they were moving into this house.

The house was far too big for two people. Now Diane would move in. Diane and Joe's dad would have children. They would be a new family and Joe wouldn't fit in.

Dad was very kind to Joe after that Saturday. He never said a word about the broken glasses or the mess. But Diane was still going to move in, there was no question about that.

Diane and Dad both explained they'd been sure he'd be pleased. They thought Joe and Diane got along so well. They'd hoped that telling him would be a celebration. They tried to get him to talk about everything, and explain why he felt so bad.

But Joe was so angry and miserable, he couldn't talk about his feelings. He told them he was OK and he would get used to the idea. He didn't make any more scenes.

So Diane moved in one day when Joe was at school. She brought all her stuff – her CD collection, her clothes, pictures, books and kitchen things – even some furniture. Wherever he looked, he saw Diane's things. Already, it seemed as if Joe didn't belong in this house any more.

"I'm hoping for the best, Joe," she said. "I like you, and I know you like me. I'm certain that this will work, and soon we'll get along well again."

Joe let her think what she wanted. But really, right from that first day she moved in, he was determined he was going to get her out.

****

At first he tried to think of cunning ways to make her and Dad split up. Maybe he could send Diane flowers and chocolates from 'a secret admirer', so Dad would think she had another boyfriend.

Then he remembered the ghost story. He knew Diane was scared of ghosts. She never watched horror movies, and she was terrified of the dark. If she believed the house was haunted, she wouldn't want to live in it.

This seemed like a better idea, less cruel than trying to break them up. Diane could go on being Dad's girlfriend, but she'd be living in her own place again. Everything would be the way it was before she moved in.

But how was he going to get her to believe the house was haunted? He'd have to be sneaky. Just telling her there was supposed to be a ghost wouldn't do much good.

Luckily, he was soon able to think of a plan, and he was sure it would work.

Chapter 4
The Ghost Tape

Joe had been interested in making sound recordings for years. He had a very good music system that his dad had bought for him on his twelfth birthday. He worked hard finding out how to create all kinds of different sound effects.

Last year the drama teacher, who knew about his hobby, had asked him to make a tape of background noises for a school play.

The tape had worked really well. The teacher had told him he'd done "an excellent professional job". Joe was proud of that. His dream was to be a sound engineer one day, and work in TV.

If Joe used his skills to make a tape of ghostly noises, it wouldn't be stupid-sounding fake groans and howls and rattling chains. He knew he could produce something truly spooky and frightening.

For days he went around trying out spooky sound effects in his head. He thought about how he would produce them and how he'd fit them together. Then he made the tape, finding times when he was alone in the house. It took hours of work, but at last he knew he had it exactly right. Now all he needed was an opportunity to test his plan.

His chance soon came. Dad had to be away overnight. In the old days Joe would have gone to stay with his mom. This time he would stay at home. Joe and Diane would be alone in the house all night.

Dad had not come back from work when Joe arrived home from school that day.

He snuck into Diane and Dad's room, loaded the tape into his old radio-alarm cassette player, and set it to start playing at 1.30 am. The player had batteries so he didn't need to plug it in.

He hid it in the back of Dad's closet, behind a row of shoes. At 1.30 am Diane would be lying in bed, either asleep or falling asleep.

The first thing she'd hear would be a series of sharp raps, like someone knocking on a door.

Then she'd hear soft footsteps, then there'd be a pause ... then the sound of someone breathing ... then another pause ... then evil muttering and rustling sounds ... More breathing, some sobbing, whimpering noises ...

And so on, for half an hour.

Joe had put some echo on the tape, and used other tricks so it would be very hard for Diane to work out where the noises were coming from. The breathing and sobbing should sound as if they were right by her, and the pauses would make it more frightening. *She'll be lying there too terrified to move*, he thought. Waiting to see if it starts up again, waiting for something worse ...

He went to bed feeling very pleased with himself. Tonight was only the beginning. He planned to hide the cassette player in different places around the house. He would load it with different mixes of his spooky effects.

Whenever Dad wasn't around, Diane would hear ghostly noises. She'd soon be a nervous wreck. She'd tell Dad, but Dad didn't believe in ghosts and he would never hear the noises, so he wouldn't believe her. She'd have to leave, and Joe would have won.

But Joe couldn't get to sleep. He kept thinking about Diane, lying there terrified. He also started thinking about his dad, and how furious he would be if he found out what Joe had done.

About midnight, he got out of bed. He'd realized that trying to scare Diane was a crazy, nasty idea that would land him in big trouble. He had to get that cassette player back. He knew Diane was still in the living room. There'd been a movie she wanted to watch on television, and it didn't finish until after midnight.

He opened his door carefully, and looked up the attic stairs. He always looked up the stairs, to see if the strange shadow was there, whenever he came out of his room. He couldn't help himself.

But this time there was no shadow. The light from his bedroom slanted upwards, into the dark. He could see the dim transparent form of a little girl in a long white night gown. She was standing with her back to him halfway up the stairs. Her brown hair was hanging down in straggly locks.

Joe felt as if the blood had drained out of him. He stepped back into his room and shut the door. He went and sat on the side of his bed. He was cold and shaking all over. He closed his hands into fists so his fingernails were digging into his palms, but he couldn't stop the shaking.

He was doomed. He was sure Dad and Diane would find out about his stupid trick, and he'd be in terrible trouble. But there was nothing he could do. There was no way, no possible way, he could leave his room while that dim figure of the girl was standing out there. He would have to turn his back on the ghost, and the thought of it made him feel sick.

In the end he managed to get back into bed. He didn't sleep much.

Chapter 5
Doomed

The next morning when he went down to breakfast, his worst fears had come true. His old radio-alarm cassette player was standing there on the breakfast bar, next to the boxes of cereal.

"I was awake half the night," said Diane, grinning at him. "Scared out of my wits, with the bedside light on. But in the morning I came to my senses, and searched the joint."

24

"Are you going to tell Dad?" asked Joe, miserably.

"Do you think I should?" said Diane.

Joe knew he should beg her not to tell his dad anything.

But she was the enemy, and he couldn't bring himself to plead for his life. So he shrugged, and said, "Do what you like. I don't care."

Diane told Joe's dad, and of course he was completely furious. When Diane saw how angry Dad was, she tried to defend Joe. She said the tape was very clever. It was only a joke. She was so glad the ghostly noises hadn't been real that she couldn't be angry with Joe.

But it was too late, the damage was done. Joe's dad grounded him for a week, but that was nothing. The way his dad looked at him was much, much worse. For days, it seemed as if they would never be friends again.

Joe had known it was going to be like this. Diane had moved in, and Joe's dad didn't belong to him any more. They were like strangers with each other. He didn't see the ghost on the stairs again. He almost managed to tell himself that he'd been imagining things.

But the wicked shadow was still there, sometimes. And sometimes, when he was alone in his room after dark, he got a weird, icy feeling. Then he knew that if he opened his door and looked up the stairs, he would see that ghostly figure again. She would have her back to him, same as before. This time she would look around, over her shoulder. He'd see her dead face peering down at him and then he was sure he would die or go mad.

Of course he never opened the door. But he felt strangely tempted. It was as if something was pulling him towards horrible destruction.

There was no one he could tell. He just had to put up with it.

He remembered that Emma had said, "if you step on the ghost's shadow you are doomed". He wondered if he'd stepped on the shadow, without knowing it. Maybe he'd trodden on the wicked shadow one night before he knew it was there when they had still been happy together. Maybe that was when everything in his life had started to go wrong.

Chapter 6
The Bricked-up Window

Gradually Dad stopped being angry. Christmas that year wasn't great for Joe, but it wasn't totally miserable either.

The weeks went by and winter passed. Joe still didn't like having Diane in the house, and hated it when she started redecorating. Every change she made seemed to be pushing Joe further away from his dad. But he knew he had to accept the situation.

When he had to be with her, he tried to behave normally. He just kept out of her way whenever he could. He spent a lot of time alone in his room. He thought about the old days and wished he could have them back.

Then his dad had to go away on another overnight trip. He told Joe about it when they were out in the garden one evening. Dad was pruning rosebushes.

Joe was wearing a pair of thick work gloves. Dad was carrying the prunings to a heap at the bottom of the garden, where he was going to make a bonfire.

Dad said, "I know you still don't get along with Diane. You've made that very clear. Do you want to go and stay with your mom that night?"

Dad didn't have to take overnight trips very often. It was the first time this had happened since the awful night of the ghostly noises.

Joe felt his cheeks turn red. He turned away so his dad wouldn't see his face.

****

It was a beautiful early spring evening. The sky was still blue, though the air was getting chilly. He could hear Diane singing as she painted the kitchen walls. The windows were open to let the paint fumes escape. She had a nice voice.

The garden of the tall, thin old house was full of bulb shoots – crocus and daffodils and tulips were popping up everywhere. They had been planted by the people who used to live here.

Joe suddenly knew how much he wanted to be happy again, even if it meant having to live with Diane. "No," he said. "That's all right. I'll stay with Diane. We'll keep each other company." It was the nearest he could come to saying he was sorry.

He looked up. The old house seemed to be leaning down over the garden, as if it was listening. Just under the roof, where the attic was, Joe saw something that he'd never noticed before. It was an outline in the brickwork that looked like a blocked up window. *That's funny*, he thought. *There aren't any bricked up windows in the attic.* But he hadn't been up there since he and Dad first moved in, so maybe he was remembering this wrong.

The funny thing was, Dad and Diane never went up to the attic either. It was as if something warned them to keep away from the haunted stairs, even though they had never seen the ghost, or the wicked shadow.

"Joe? What's up?"

He realized that his dad had been trying to hand him another bundle of rose prunings, and Joe had been standing there ignoring him.

"Nothing," said Joe. "I was daydreaming."

Chapter 7
The Storm

The next morning Joe's dad came down to breakfast with his overnight bag already packed. His trip would last two days. Joe and Diane wouldn't see him until late the next evening.

His dad said, "You have my cell phone number, in case anything goes wrong." Then he gave Diane a kiss and Joe a hug. "Look after my girl for me," he said to Joe. "I'm depending on you."

Joe nodded, and smiled as best he could. He felt as if he was on trial.

It was a Tuesday. Joe had soccer training after school, so it was past five o'clock by the time he came home.

Diane was already back from work. She was out in the garden, looking up at the sky. The day had been strangely warm. Now there were heavy clouds, the color of bruises, gathering overhead.

"I think we're going to have a thunderstorm," she said.

"Can you have thunderstorms in February?" asked Joe. He thought thunder belonged in summer.

"I don't know, but it looks like we're going to get one," said Diane.

They went indoors. "Should I cook some dinner for both of us," said Diane, "or would you rather order a pizza?"

Joe remembered when he and his dad used to do the cooking together. It hurt to think that time was over forever. He didn't mind eating meals Diane had cooked when Dad was here. But if she cooked for him when Dad wasn't here, it would be like admitting she'd taken over. It would be a big defeat. But he swallowed his pride.

"If you feel like cooking, there's not much point in getting a pizza," he mumbled.

"Great. How about burgers and fries?" offered Diane.

"That's not very healthy," said Joe.

"I know, but I'm sure you had a healthy lunch," said Diane, with a mischievous grin. "Let's give ourselves a night off from being sensible."

While Joe had a shower to wash off the soccer mud, Diane cooked. They ate together at the kitchen table. By the time they'd finished eating, rain was rattling on the kitchen windows.

As Joe got up to put the plates in the sink there was a low, soft rumble in the distance.

"Thunder," said Diane, uneasily. "I was right."

When he'd done the dishes, Joe went off to his own room to do his homework. But he never had much homework on a Tuesday.

After he'd finished it, he sat staring at the wall above his desk. The thunder was getting closer, and the rain and wind sounded wild. It was a powerful storm.

He thought about Diane, downstairs, alone. He knew she was frightened of thunderstorms. He sighed. It was no use. He'd have to go and keep her company. They could watch television, so he wouldn't have to talk to her.

"Hello," he said as he walked into the living room. "I finished my homework. What's on?"

"Hi," said Diane. "N-nothing much. There's a movie on later that might be good."

Joe sat down. They watched the news together, but did not say much to each other. That was the good thing about Diane, she never chattered for the sake of talking.

Joe began to relax. He found himself remembering how he used to like her, before she moved in.

Suddenly, they heard several loud raps. The sounds didn't come from the front door. They were very close.

Joe nearly jumped out of his skin. He stared at Diane, and she stared back at him.

They heard soft footsteps pattering, as if they were right here in the living room.

"I'm not doing it!" yelled Joe, "It's not me! I'm not playing tricks!" Joe thought somehow the spooky tape must have turned itself on. But he didn't know where it was. He hadn't seen his old radio-alarm player since he'd played that trick on Diane. His dad had kept it.

He jumped up, looking around wildly.

The rapping started again, mixed with sounds like a child sobbing. The hairs on the back of Joe's neck stood on end, and he had that horrible icy feeling.

"I'm not doing it!" he repeated, desperately, "It's not me!"

"I know," gasped Diane, her eyes huge with fear. "Joe, don't worry, I ..."

Whatever else she said was lost in a great crash of thunder.

The television picture vanished, and all the lights went out.

Chapter 8
Maisie Day

Diane grabbed Joe's hand. Together they stumbled to the kitchen. It was completely dark in there. The wind howled and the rain at the windows sounded like machine gun fire. Another huge clap of thunder was followed by a vivid bolt of lightning.

For a flash of a second Joe saw Diane scrabbling in a kitchen drawer. Then the kitchen was black again, but she'd found some candles and some matches. She lit two candles and put them on the kitchen counter.

Now they could see each other – two frightened faces surrounded by darkness.

The raps came again, and the sobbing. The noises seemed to be here in the kitchen.

"Joe," said Diane, breathlessly. "I believe you. I know you're not playing tricks. Your dad destroyed that tape, and I'm sure you wouldn't do that again, anyway."

"Then what's going on?" gasped Joe.

"This is supposed to be a haunted house," said Diane, "I always knew that."

"You knew?" whispered Joe.

"Yes," said Diane.

They each took a candle and sat down on the floor. Their backs were against the doors of the kitchen cabinets. They did not dare to move from the spot.

"It started a hundred years ago," began Diane. "There was a terrible epidemic of scarlet fever in the town. A little girl, called Maisie Day, was living in this house. She was eight years old. She caught the fever. Scarlet fever was a very dangerous disease, then. Her mom and dad put her in a room by herself, so she wouldn't infect the other children ..."

Joe gulped. He thought, *I've seen her!* But he couldn't bring himself to say that out loud, he was too scared. "Why didn't they send her to a hospital?" he asked.

"They were too poor. They had a lot of children. People had big families in those days. Maisie had four little brothers and sisters. Her father took the two older ones to stay with their grandmother in the country. Her mother stayed, with the baby and the toddler, and Maisie.

"But then Maisie's mother caught the fever herself. No one really knows what happened after that. The neighbors took Maisie's mother to a charity hospital, and looked after the little ones.

"Apparently everyone thought Maisie had gone with her father, and her mother was too sick to tell them the truth. So Maisie Day was left behind. And the door to her room was locked. Her mother had kept it locked, so the toddler wouldn't run in there and catch the fever."

"S-so ..." whispered Joe, his voice shaking. "W-what happened to her?"

"She died, Joe. Her mother and father found her dead in that room when they came back. No one knows which room it was. But ever since then, the people who've lived in this house – not all of them, just some of them – have heard her crying in the night and hammering on a locked door."

Diane took hold of Joe's hand. "That's why I was so scared by your tape," she explained. "Because I knew the story of poor Maisie Day. But I would never have told your dad about that trick you played on me, if I had known how angry he'd be. I just didn't think. I've wanted to tell you I was sorry about that."

"I thought it would make you move out, because you were afraid of ghosts," said Joe.

"I *am* afraid," said Diane. "Maybe your dad is, too. Maybe that's why he was so angry. But Joe, think about it. She's only a little girl."

Diane stood up. "If a lost child cries like that, it's because she wants to be found. Come on, let's go and find her."

Chapter 9
Fear in the Dark

All the time Joe and Diane been talking, there had been no noise but the raging of the storm. As Diane stood up, a whimpering sound seemed to come from outside in the hall.

"Let's take flashlights," said Joe. He didn't like the look of his candle's flickering flame. He felt sure it would go out.

He found two flashlights in another drawer. They took the candles and matches with them as well and set off. They followed the ghostly noises. It was like a very scary game of hide-and-seek. When they were on the landing outside Diane and Dad's room, they heard pattering footsteps come up behind them.

When they turned around there was nothing. As they looked into Joe's room, the rapping started again downstairs. When they hurried towards that sound, something started muttering and sobbing by the kitchen door ...

There were other sounds too. The worst was a kind of scrabbling and gnawing that gave Joe horrible ideas – about rats and a sick, little girl who couldn't get away.

They crept from room to room, trying every light switch to see if the power had come back on, but it hadn't.

Joe didn't know why he was doing this. He thought Diane's plan was crazy. But anything was better than cowering helplessly in the dark, waiting for something horrible to happen.

As they came upstairs for the third time Joe distinctly heard soft, rapid breathing right by his ear. He was sure that something passed him, heading for the attic. He didn't think Diane had heard anything, but this time she wanted to go up there.

"No!" said Joe. He was too scared.

Diane didn't argue. Maybe she felt the same as Joe, as she stood at the bottom of those narrow dark stairs. Only a fool would dare to go ghost-chasing up there.

They went back to the living room. There was still no power and the storm thundered on.

For what seemed like a long time, nothing happened. Joe remembered how he'd put pauses between the spooky effects on that stupid tape, to make it more scary. He'd been right about that, he decided.

Then a hand touched his arm. It was a small hand so cold he could feel it like a grip of ice, through the sleeve of his sweater. He turned his head, terrified of what he might see but unable not to look ...

Diane was sitting beside him, holding her flashlight in both hands. She was staring at the circle of light it made on the rug.

Beyond Diane, in the open doorway of the room, a strange light that came from nowhere showed him the figure of a girl in a white nightdress. She had her back to him.

Chapter 10
Maisie's Room

Joe had no choice. He couldn't resist. The
ghost had come to fetch him and he had to
follow. Out into the hall, up the stairs ... and
on, up to the attic.

The wild sounds of the storm continued,
and the light of his flashlight had turned
yellow and feeble. The batteries were running
out. He desperately wanted to turn back, but
he couldn't. He pressed himself against the

wall, as he climbed those narrow stairs. He was afraid to step on the place where that wicked shadow lay.

Now nothing could save him. He'd reached the door to the attic.

He had to turn the doorknob, open the door and look in. He tried to switch on the light, but nothing happened. His feeble flashlight beam showed an empty dusty space.

The ghost stood facing the wall, with her brown hair hanging down. In a moment she would turn and look at him over her shoulder. He would see her dead face.

Joe started to scream. He screamed and screamed. Footsteps came pounding up the narrow stairs ...

"Joe!" cried Diane, "What's happening? Why did you leave me like that?"

He couldn't speak. He grabbed at her, forgetting all his pride.

Diane hugged him hard. "It's OK," she told him, sounding terrified but very brave. "Don't worry, it's OK …"

At that moment, wonderfully, the light came on. Diane sighed with relief, and looked around. There were two attic rooms. This was the bigger one. It was completely empty. "What happened, Joe? Did you see something?"

"Look!" croaked Joe, pointing with a shaking hand.

Diane shook her head. "I can't see anything." She went to the place where he was

pointing, and looked at the wall. "Joe!" she
exclaimed, "I think there was a door here!"

Diane could see nothing, but Joe could still
see the dim figure of a little girl. "Don't!" he
whispered, horrified. "Don't touch her!"

He watched, paralyzed, as the girl's tousled,
brown head started to turn. He imagined the
hollow cheeks and empty stare of the little girl
who had been left alone to die. But he did not
see her face. Diane was in the way. Or maybe,
at the last moment, he managed to close his
eyes.

When he looked again, Diane had passed
through the ghost, and the girl was gone.
Diane was tearing ruthlessly at the faded
wallpaper. The plaster underneath fell off in
chunks and revealed the corner of a lock, on
the door of a hidden room – perhaps a room
that had been hidden for a hundred years?

I think we've found the place where Maisie Day died," said Diane. She looked solemn but then she smiled at Joe. "We'll come back in daylight, and open it up. It's all right, don't be scared. I'm sure this is what she wanted us to find. I'm sure the haunting is over." She laughed. "I'd better call your dad. He'll be worried. He knows I hate thunderstorms."

In fact it was the next Saturday before they forced the door open. The small room inside was very bare. There was a window that had been bricked up. And there was a bed – a little iron-framed bed. In the ancient, dusty, rotten mattress that lay on the frame, you could still see the hollow imprint of a child's body.

There was nothing else in the room.

Diane said she was going to get the window opened up again. She planned to clean the hidden room out and decorate. They would use it for something happy and good. She was sure that was the best way to heal the memory of that long ago tragedy.

Maybe Joe and his dad could have a computer station and workshop up there together.

Joe's dad didn't believe in ghosts, but he agreed with her.

There couldn't be any harm in using that room.

Joe hoped they were right.